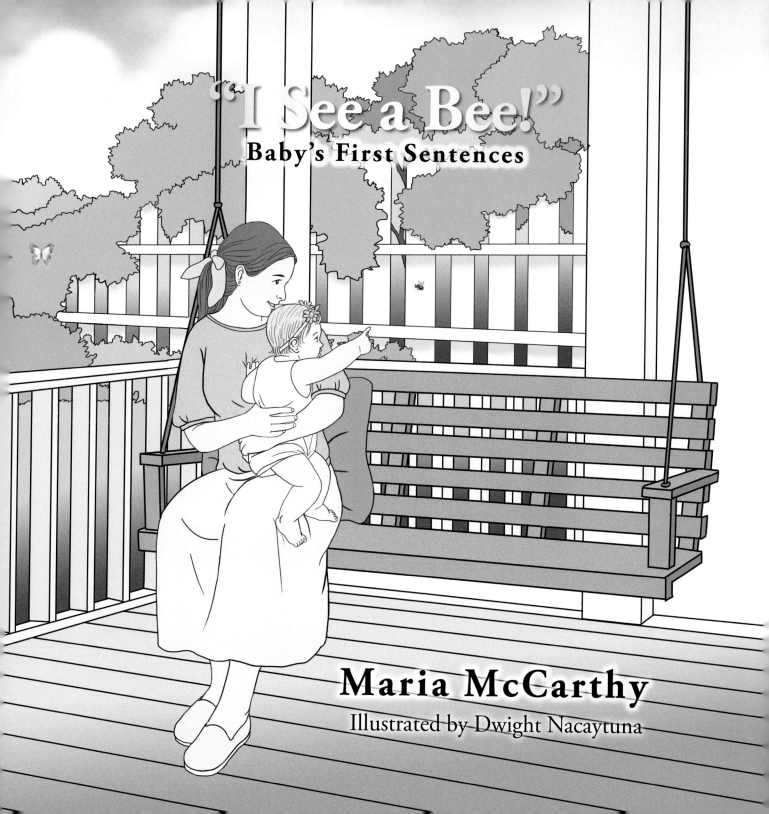

"I See a Bee!"
Baby's First Sentences

Maria McCarthy

Illustrated by Dwight Nacaytuna

To order additional copies of this book, contact:
Xlibris
1-888-795-4274
www.Xlibris.com
Orders@Xlibris.com

"I See a Bee!"

Baby's First Sentences

"I see a bee!"

Owls perch on trees.

Bears eat honey.

The snail hides under the leaf.

"Look at the sky!" There is much to see.

"I see balloons."

"I see the moon. I see stars."

"I see you!" says baby.

"I love you," says Mama.

What do

you see?

"McCarthy has written a deceivingly simple, straightforward, engaging, and colorful children's book for beginners. And it is one which, above all else, will bring out the joy in young early readers, as they begin themselves to sound out the individual word and, with repeated practice, the entire book of short sentences."

- Jonah Meyer,
The US Review of Books

Printed in the United States
By Bookmasters